Humble Heroes

By Linda Halliday   Illustrated by Cheryl Crout

Published in Chicago, Illinois

Printed in the United States

ISBN: 979-8-9889283-0-0

Library of Congress Control Number: 2023915344

Dedicated to the students that made storytime the best
moments of the teaching day
and
McHenry Township Fire Protection District in support of
their mission to keep their community safe

Oreo and Luna were best friends. Oreo was older and wiser than Luna and was always teaching her important things.

"Luna, it's a bad idea to chase balls on a slippery floor. And barking at the vacuum is a waste of time," said Oreo.

After lunch, Oreo took a nap. Luna followed Mom around the house. Luna saw colorful balloons. She smelled cake. Mom put candles and matches on the counter. Wrapped presents were on the table. "What is going on?" Luna wondered.

Ding-dong! The doorbell rang loudly. Luna barked and barked. Children were arriving for a birthday party! While Mom was rushing to answer the door, she accidently knocked the matches onto the floor. Luna saw them fall, but got distracted by the excitement.

After getting hugs from Donny and Jaelyn, Luna remembered the matches on the floor. She knew children should never touch matches or lighters. Luna's Mom visited schools to talk about safety, and one time Luna got to go with her! Mom told the students that if they found matches or lighters, they should tell an adult right away. Mom said matches and lighters can get hot, and playing with them can cause a fire, or getting hurt with a painful burn.

"But I'm only a little dog," Luna thought to herself. "What could I do?"

"I know! I'll ask Oreo!" Luna found Oreo curled up in a ball. "Oreo, wake up," whispered Luna, as she gently pawed Oreo's head. Oreo slowly opened one eye.

Oreo mumbled, "Go jump on Mom. That will get her attention." Then Oreo yawned, rolled over, and promptly went back to sleep.

"Oreo's right! I need to get Mom's attention to let her know about the matches!" Luna ran downstairs and jumped on Mom's leg, but Mom kindly told Luna she was too busy to play. Luna was frustrated.

This time when Luna found Oreo, she heard snoring. Since Oreo said jumping on people got attention, Luna jumped on Oreo. "Yikes!" yelled Oreo. Oreo was not happy to be woken up like that! Still, while fixing her doggie bed, Oreo offered more advice.

"Try pretending you see a squirrel," said Oreo, knowing that Luna always made a fool of herself when she saw squirrels. That would get Mom's attention!

Luna found Mom. She yelped and spun in silly circles! Mom looked at Luna, then out the window. She did not see a squirrel. Mom was confused. "What should I do now?" wondered Luna.

This time, Luna found Oreo sleeping on her back. Oreo's paws were twitching. Oreo was dreaming of a big dog bone.

Following Oreo's latest idea, Luna pretended a squirrel was there. "Ahhh!" screamed Oreo. At first, Oreo thought this excitement meant people were sharing their food with dogs, which is the only important reason to wake up right away according to Oreo.

"I still have a lot to teach this little one," she thought.

Oreo decided a big drink of water was needed first.
But, the bowl was empty!

Luna watched while Oreo stretched, took a deep breath, then let out the loudest barks ever! "Woof, woof!"

Since Oreo only barked when it was really important, as wise dogs do, Mom came over right away.

Oreo looked at Mom, moved her head to look at the empty bowl, then looked back at Mom. Mom understood! She picked up the empty bowl and filled it with water.

"I have an idea!" thought Luna. She ran to the matches. She stretched, took a deep breath, then let out the loudest barks she could. "Arf! Arf!"

When Mom came over, Luna looked at the matches, then at Mom, then at the matches again. Mom understood! She picked up the matches and put them away in a high, safe place! Luna was filled with joy!

Then Mom looked at Luna and said, "Is this what you have been trying to tell me all along? Good girl, Luna!"

Luna wagged her tail so hard that her whole body wiggled. Mom gave Luna pets. Then Mom scratched Oreo's head. "You're a good girl, too, Oreo." Luna had learned from Oreo after all.

"Now how about a treat for my two good girls?" asked Mom. Oreo sat down and lifted her paw. Mom gave Oreo a big bone.

Luna was still wagging her tail wildly. Mom gave Luna a little bone.

Later, after everyone sang the birthday song, Luna was happily perched on Mom's lap at the adults' table, with a slice of cake a few doggie paws away. Luna looked at the cake with big, hopeful eyes. It looked delicious!

In the meantime, the older and wiser Oreo had chosen to hang out under the kids' table. Oreo was already enjoying the cake. It tasted delicious indeed!

FIRE SAFETY TIPS

1) Keep matches and lighters in a high place, out of children's reach. Teach your children not to touch matches or lighters and to tell an adult if they find them. For children under the age of 5, fireplay is the leading cause of fire death. Resources: *National Fire Protection Association*: nfpa.org

2) Sleep with bedroom doors closed. Doing so keeps toxic smoke and carbon monoxide from the room longer, reduces soaring temperatures, and helps stop the spread of fire. Resources: closeyourdoor.org

3) Install a smoke alarm on every floor of your home and outside all sleeping areas. Test smoke alarms once a month. nfpa.org

4) Install a carbon monoxide alarm on each floor of the home, and one outside of sleeping areas. nfpa.org

5) Make and practice a home fire escape plan. Downloadable plan at: nfpa.org

6) For fire safety games, videos, and activities for various ages of children: sparky.org

7) Activities for kids, teens, families, educators, and organizations: ready.gov/kids

8) Smokey the Bear teaches about preventing wildfires with games and activities: smokeybear.com

Free PAWsom PALS story resources for parents and educators:
www.pawsompals.com
10% of book sale proceeds will be donated - see website for organizations

Linda Halliday (Willetts) is a former teacher, and public safety educator for a fire department.These experiences inspired the intention to teach children through entertaining stories. Her love of dogs, their silly antics, and unique personalities are the heart of PAWsom PALS.

In her free time, she enjoys the outdoors, taking the dogs on adventures, and reading. Linda volunteers at a local elementary school helping students who need extra support learning to read.

Oreo

Luna

Made in the USA
Monee, IL
20 March 2024